# MARTHA SPEAKS™

# Teacher's Pet

Adaptation by Jamie White

Based on TV series teleplays
written by Pippin Parker and Silvia Olivas

Based on characters created by Susan Meddaugh

HOUGHTON MIFFLIN HARCOURT
Boston · New York

For information about permission to reproduce selections from this book, write to Permissions, Houghton Mifflin Harcourt Publishing Company, 215 Park Avenue South, New York, New York 10003.

ISBN: 978-0-544-22798-9 hardcover
ISBN: 978-0-544-22797-2 paperback

Cover design by Rachel Newborn | Book design by Bill Smith Studio

www.hmhco.com | www.marthathetalkingdog.com

Manufactured in China | SCP 10 9 8 7 6 5 4 3 2 1 | 4500476084

# MARTHA 101

Ahem. May I have your attention, please? It's Martha, here to teach you all about a fascinating subject—guess who?

But first, a pop quiz. Complete this sentence: Martha is a . . .

a. former detective, radio talk show host, fire dog, and teacher

b. hero who once saw a burglar break in to her house and called 911 to save the day

c. talking dog

d. all of the above

If you guessed d, then you get an A!

You see, ever since my owner Helen fed me her alphabet soup, I've been able to speak. And speak and speak . . . No one's sure how or why, but the letters in the soup traveled up to my brain instead of down to my stomach.

Now, as long as I eat my daily bowl of alphabet soup, I can talk. To my family—Helen, baby Jake, Mom, Dad, and our nontalking dog, Skits. To Helen's best human friend, T.D. To anyone who'll listen, really.

*But, Martha,* you might be wondering, *how does your family feel about living with a*

*chatty dog?* Well, they sometimes wish I didn't talk *quite* so much.

But my speaking comes in handy. Like when I lent a paw to help Alice with her Spanish homework. Or when I taught Helen's class. Although, that didn't work out *exactly* as planned.

Listen up and I'll tell you all about it. You're about to learn how a dog becomes a teacher.

Our lesson begins when Helen's real teacher, Mrs. Clusky, made an announcement . . .

# MARTHA LESSON #5

"Attention, students!" said Mrs. Clusky.

As usual, T.D. was doodling in his notebook.

"*Attention* means you should focus and listen carefully to what I'm going to say," said Mrs. Clusky. "*T.D.!*"

His head shot up. "Right," he said. "Attention. Listening carefully."

"Thank you," said Mrs. Clusky. "First, tomorrow your reports on animal behavior are due."

"Animal behavior? That sounds *ruff!*" T.D. barked.

The class giggled.

"*And,*" said Mrs. Clusky, "I'm going to be away for the rest of the week, so another teacher will be taking my place."

Helen and T.D. exchanged uneasy glances. That day, he doodled a new picture. He shared it with Helen on their walk home.

"I'M YOUR SUBSTITUTE!" T.D. shouted, holding up his drawing of a fire-breathing teacher. "FEAR ME!"

"Nice," said Helen. "What do you think our substitute will really be like?"

"Based on history?" he replied. "I'd say weird."

"You mean like the yeller?" Helen asked, remembering the substitute who shouted like a drill sergeant.

"Or the smeller?" T.D. said. "She kept sniffing her sandwich."

"Or the tapper," said Helen, recalling the teacher who tapped his desk all day.

"Or the rapper!" they cried together.

T.D. laughed. "Remember how he introduced himself?"

"'My name is Mister Hendricks. It's time for attendance!'" rapped Helen.

"You know who I'd like for a substitute?" T.D. asked. "A robot!" He moved his arms stiffly

and said in a flat voice, "Today-instead-of-normal-homework-you-will-construct-a-rocket-propelled-snowboard."

Helen collapsed in giggles on the front steps. That's when I ran up to greet her.

"You're home!" I cried, racing into her arms. I ran welcome-home-Helen laps around the yard.

"Hey! Do you know who would be a great substitute?" T.D. asked her. "Martha!"

"Can you imagine?" said Helen. "First lesson: The dog paddle."

"Second lesson: Catch tennis balls with our teeth," T.D. added.

"Third lesson: Dig for bones," said Helen.

"Fourth lesson: Lap water from the toilet," said T.D.

Helen wrinkled her nose. "Ew."

"What?" I said. "Drinking from the toilet is an invaluable skill. Especially if you don't have hands."

But T.D. wasn't listening. He'd just noticed a slip of paper in his book.

"Whoa," he said, picking it up. "Check it out!"

"What is it?" Helen asked.

"It's the sign-up sheet for substitute teachers," he replied. "I must have grabbed it from my mom's stuff by mistake."

"Is it weird having your mom be our school vice principal?" Helen asked.

"Nah. I just pretend not to know her," said T.D. He scribbled something on the paper and held it up for Helen to see. "Did I spell Martha's name right?"

Helen's eyes bugged. "You're *really* signing her up as a teacher?"

"Just as a goof," said T.D. "It would never really happen."

Fifth lesson: When it comes to talking dogs, never say never.

# THE PHONE CALL

That evening, I was doing the usual—eating alphabet soup—when the phone rang. I padded down the hall to answer it. Big mistake!

"Hello?" I said.

"Thank heavens I reached you," a woman answered. "Is this Martha Lorraine?"

"That's right," I replied.

"This is Mrs. Clusky from the school," she said. "I'm so glad you're around. The other

substitutes were all sick. So you're going to substitute for me tomorrow."

"I am?"

"That's right," she said.

"But a substitute is something that takes the place of something else, right?" I said.

"Right, but—"

"Like, if you don't have a ball to play with, you can use a stick for a substitute?" I said.

"Right, so—"

"So we're going to play fetch?" I cried, wagging my tail. "YES!"

Mrs. Clusky sighed. "No. I'm a *teacher*, and you're going to be my substitute when I'm away."

"Okay," I said hesitantly.

"Don't worry," she said. "The students are well behaved, and—"

A car horn honked in the background.

"I have to go!" she said hurriedly. "Do you have any questions? No? Thanks! Bye!" *Click*.

"Uh . . ." I said to a dial tone.

Helen found me staring at the phone.

"Everything okay?" she asked.

"I think so," I said. "What are you studying in Mrs. Clusky's class?"

"Animal behavior," said Helen, hanging up the phone. "Why?"

But I'd already disappeared into the kitchen.

"Animal behavior? No wonder she called me," I said. "Just think, two minutes ago I was your average, everyday talking dog, and now look at me!" I stepped onto the table and stood tall. "A teacher! A revered member of that most noble of professions. A—"

"Martha!" Helen scolded from the doorway. "Off the table!"

Sigh. Teachers are such an underappreciated breed.

The next morning, I was bursting with excitement as I reached the school steps.

"My first day as a teacher!" I said to myself. "I can almost feel a newfound sense of respect in the air."

Just then, I heard a voice. "HEY, MUTT!" a man hollered.

I looked up to see the school janitor at

the top of the steps. Surely he wasn't talking to me!

"Yeah, *you!*" he snarled. "Shoo! You're not allowed in school. See? NO DOGS."

He pointed to a sign showing a picture of a dog with a red slash through it.

"But that dog doesn't look anything like me," I said, inching forward.

19

"Not one step closer," he warned, jabbing his mop toward me. "Or I'll douse you with dirty mop water."

*Hey! What's the big woof?* I thought, backing away. *I'm just a dog. Going to school. To teach humans.*

Meanwhile, the clock was ticking. Helen's class was beginning to wonder where their substitute was.

"Who do you think it will be?" Helen asked Alice.

"Whoever it is," she replied, "they're late."

# TEACHER'S PET

I trotted alongside the building, wondering where to go. I couldn't go home with my tail between my legs. Teachers don't let their students down. Teachers are heroes!

Then I noticed something on the first floor. An open window!

I leapt through it. *Oof!* Now that, my friends, is called dogged determination. I'd landed in

the hallway near Helen's classroom door. What luck!

"Hello," I said, strolling inside. "My name is Martha. I'm your substitute teacher."

The class gasped.

"Martha?!" Helen cried. She spun toward T.D. "Can you believe it? A plan of yours actually worked!"

"Wow," T.D. whispered, in awe. "I promise to use this newfound power only for good."

I leapt onto the teacher's chair. "Let's see. The first thing we'll do is, um . . ."

I had no idea. Dogs don't take tests; we take naps. Thankfully, Helen raised her hand.

"Yes! Helen!" I called.

"We start the day by taking attendance," she said.

"Uh . . . attendance?" I replied.

"Attending school means to be at school," she explained. "Attendance is when you read out our names to see who's here and who's absent."

"Oh, *attendance!*" I said. "But why waste time reading all those names? Everyone who's here today, say 'present.'"

"PRESENT!" the kids said in chorus.

"Everyone who's not here, say 'Absent.'"

The room was silent.

"Perfect. Nobody's absent," I said.

In the back of the room, T.D. whispered to Helen, "Her methods are unusual and make no sense."

"I heard that, T.D.," I said. "I hear everything."

I jumped down and paced in front of my desk.

"Now," I said, "I understand you've been studying animal behavior. Who are these animals? What are their names? Maybe I'm friends with them."

The kids stared blankly.

"Who wants to go first?" I asked. "Helen?"

She held up some pages. "We have these reports we did for homework. For you to, uh, *read*."

I gulped. Read? I don't know how to read!
"New plan," I said quickly. "Instead of me reading your homework, you read your reports to me."

"You mean like an oral report?" Helen said.

"Huh?"

"Reports that are read aloud," Helen said.

"Very good," I said. "Who's first?"

"I'll go," Alice volunteered.

She read her report in front of the class. "So," she said, "because chameleons can hide

themselves by changing colors, they're one of the world's most amazing animals."

I yawned. Chameleons, shameleons. "Okay. If you say so," I said. "Who's next? Helen?"

Alice looked deflated as Helen took her place.

"My report is about the behavior of cats," said Helen.

"*Cats?*" I cried. "How do you expect to get a good grade if you write a report on cats?"

"That's not fair," said Helen. "Just because you don't like them . . ."

True. I dislike cats as much as the janitor disliked me. The janitor, who at that moment was hot on my trail. He'd just spotted something I'd left on the hallway floor . . .

"Is that what I think it is?" he said, bending down to take a closer look. Using tweezers, he picked up the evidence and held it to the light.

"Yup," he said, narrowing his eyes. "*Dog* hair."

# TODAY'S LESSON: DOGS ARE COOL

On his hands and knees, the janitor followed my trail down the hall. He was getting close. Too close. Until a pair of sensible shoes blocked his path.

"I've been looking all over for you," said Mrs. Kennelly. "We have an emergency!"

He stood up and held out my hair. "A *dog* emergency, right?"

"Someone threw up in the art room," she said.

"Is it . . ." said the janitor, "*dog* throw-up?"

Mrs. Kennelly sighed.

Meanwhile, I was teaching just a room away. "I think we've heard all we need to hear about cats," I said to Helen. "Who's next? T.D.?"

Helen shuffled to her seat, looking as disappointed as Alice.

"Okay," said T.D., walking to my desk. "I don't exactly have the written report with me because I forgot to write it. But mine is about the behavior of, um . . ." His eyes searched the room until they landed on me. "Oh, dogs! My subject is dogs."

"Finally!" I exclaimed. "I mean, er, excellent choice."

"Dogs are . . . hairy," he said. "Although, then again, some aren't."

"True," I said. "But behavior isn't what an animal or person looks like. Behavior is how they act. What they do."

"Right," said T.D. "I was getting to that. Dogs are cool."

Much better," I said.

"They have a good sense of smell," he continued. "They're trustworthy."

"Loyal," I added.

"Helpful."

"Friendly, courteous, and kind."

"Obedient and cheerful," T.D. said.

"Brave, sweet-smelling, and—"

"Fun!" T.D. exclaimed.

"Fantastic!" I said. "Let's all give T.D. a big dog thanks for a job well done."

The students clapped.

"Not like that. Like this!" I said, leaping onto my desk. "Jump up, wag your tail, and bark with delight. *Woof!* Class participation! Everyone join in!"

The class did as instructed. *"Woof! Woof! Woof!"*

"Now you're behaving like dogs!" I said. "Now jump up and lick his face! Everyone!"

I was bounding toward T.D. when a faint sound made me freeze.

"Hold it!" I ordered. "Someone's at the door."

The janitor's scowling face appeared in the door's window. Uh-oh. He'd found me! He pointed, as if to say *I've got you now, mutt!* Then, mysteriously, he disappeared.

"Whoa," said T.D. "How did you hear that?"

"Don't you remember me telling you?" I said, getting back on my chair. "We dogs have an

amazing sense of hearing and smell. That's why we're used for search-and-rescue teams. Write this down. There'll be a test on it tomorrow."

Suddenly, the janitor burst in with Mrs. Kennelly behind him.

"A-HA!" he cried to her. "You see? A DOG!"

"Problem?" I asked.

"Yes, I see," Mrs. Kennelly said to him. "I see a well-behaved class paying attention to the lesson." She strolled over to me. "Hi, Martha! Hi, T.D.!"

T.D. blushed. "Uh, hi, Mom."

"Now, is that how we learned to greet someone, T.D.?" I said. "Jump up! Give your mom a loud *woof woof woof!*"

T.D. reluctantly got up on his desk. "*Woof woof woof.*"

"Today's lesson is about animal behavior," I explained to Mrs. Kennelly.

"Class participation?" she said. "How fun! Did T.D. tell you about my famous imitation of Courageous Collie Carlo saving a baby frog?"

"Ooh! My favorite dog actor!" I said. "Let's see."

"NO! Mom, please!" T.D. begged.

But Mrs. Kennelly was already on the floor, barking. *"Woof woof woof!"*

"Stop! I beg you!" T.D. pleaded. He covered his eyes as his mom hopped across the floor. *"Ribbit ribbit!"* she croaked.

The class laughed.

"Excellent imitation, Mrs. Kennelly," I said.

"Thanks, Martha," she said. "I love your teaching techniques. We're so lucky to have you."

But as T.D. slid under his desk in embarrassment, I wondered if the kids felt the same.

# AN EARLY RETIREMENT

Walking home from school, T.D. gazed wistfully at the monster teacher he'd drawn.

"Now I wish we *had* gotten this substitute," he said to Helen.

She nodded. "Martha didn't like anyone's report but yours," she said. "And that's just

because it was about dogs. Now everyone's blaming *me* because Martha's my pet."

"Well, at least you didn't watch your mother imitate Courageous Collie Carlo in front of the whole class," T.D. said.

Helen winced. "You got me there."

At home, she plopped down on the couch to watch TV.

"Don't you have homework to do, young lady?" I asked, peeking into the living room.

"Gah!" Helen cried. She got up and stomped past me.

"What's the matter?" I asked, following her out of the room.

"I thought it would be *fun* having you for a teacher . . ." she said.

Oh, no. This wasn't working out the way I wanted. I missed the way things were. Like how I'd greet her after school, and how she'd hug me. I had to fix things. But how?

Then I had an idea.

The next morning, I asked the class for their attention.

"I have an announcement," I said, looking at Helen. "Actually, it's more like an oral report. Yesterday, I made someone I care for unhappy, and—"

My ears perked up. Someone was by the door. *Not that janitor again!* I thought.

But when the door burst open, a woman in glasses appeared instead. Mrs. Clusky!

"I'm back!" she sang, and sighed in relief. "I couldn't stay away from all of you. Also, I had a dream you'd all grown tails and fur."

"Oh, Mrs. Clusky!" said Mrs. Kennelly, peeking into the room. "We weren't expecting you back so soon. You'll be happy to know that Martha did an excellent job teaching your class."

Mrs. Clusky's jaw dropped. "*Martha?* Martha Lorraine is . . . *you*, Martha?"

"Yes," I confessed, "but I think my teaching days are over."

"Are you sure?" asked Mrs. Kennelly.

"Oh, I'm sure," I said, heading for the door. "In the end, being a teacher is no substitute for being a friend."

Behind me came Helen's voice. "Hey, Martha?" she said.

I turned around to see her smiling.

"See you at home!" she said.

Next to her, T.D. got up on his desk. *"Woof!"* he barked.

I wagged my tail. *"Woof!"*

"Bye, Martha!" the class sang. "We'll miss you!"

I'd miss them, too. But I had to admit, I was looking forward to catching up on important business back home. Like chasing squirrels . . . and eating from the trash . . . and hanging out at the fire hydrant. Ahh, I love the dog life!

At the school's exit, the janitor was waiting. *Uh-oh,* I thought. *What now?*

But to my surprise, he opened the door.

"Thanks," I said.

"Oh, I wasn't opening it for you," he replied gruffly. "I just, uh, wanted some fresh air." He sniffed. "Okay, that's enough."

"My thoughts exactly," I said, and raced into the sunshine.

# ALICE'S SECRET

Now that my teaching career was over, I thought I was done with school for good.

I was wrong.

You see, the kids thought a talking dog could help them with Spanish homework. Isn't that *loco*? I don't even speak Spanish!

It all started after their teacher, Señor Craig, handed back their quizzes. Helen aced it. T.D. wasn't as fortunate.

"Aww, man!" he cried when he saw his grade. "How did that happen?"

"I don't know, *amigo*," said Señor Craig. "Did you study?"

T.D. slapped his forehead. "Gah! I knew I forgot something."

Next up was Alice. She received a D.

"Ugh!" she groaned.

"So this isn't your best grade either," said Señor Craig. "But don't worry, Alicia. Our next

assignment will help you articulate better in Spanish."

"Articulate? What's that mean?" she asked.

"The North Pole didn't come to work on time?" T.D. offered. "Get it? Arctic, like the North Pole? 'Arctic, you late!'"

"Not quite," said Señor Craig. "To articulate is to say something clearly. But this assignment is like the Arctic in one way—it's really cool."

The kids didn't agree. They grumped about it all the way home.

"An oral report in *Spanish?*" Alice whined.

"There's nothing cool about that," said T.D. "*Nada.*"

"An oral report in *Spanish?*" Alice repeated.

"What's the matter?" Helen asked. "You pronounce everything perfectly in Spanish."

"Uh-uh," said Alice. "When you pronounce something, you say it. I never say a word in class."

"But you do!" said Helen. "I remember on the first day, you said '*buenos días*' perfectly."

T.D. giggled, remembering how Alice had shouted each word. "Your voice was *loud*," he said.

Alice cringed. "Well, I can't seem to learn any other Spanish. I certainly can't speak in front of everyone. *Buenos días* is the only Spanish I know."

She imagined how her report would go. She'd stand there repeating *buenos días* a bazillion different ways . . .

"*Buenos días,*" she'd say, followed by a cheerful "*¡Buenos días!, ¿Buenos días?*" Then she'd wrap it up with a firm "*Buenos días. The end.*"

She pictured Señor Craig shaking his head.

"*Buenos días,*" she'd say sadly.

*Ay-ay-ay.* Alice was in *mucho* trouble.

The kids continued their conversation at our house over ice cream. I stood near the table. Not because I care about Spanish, but because I care deeply about ice cream.

Alice rested her head on the table.

"C'mon," said T.D. "You know more Spanish than *buenos días*."

"Yeah. You're always raising your hand in class," said Helen.

"Not exactly," said Alice. "Whenever Señor Craig calls for answers, I only raise my hand *after* he calls on someone else."

Helen and T.D. were confused.

"What about when he asks you to read aloud?" Helen asked.

"I pretend to have laryngitis," Alice replied. "Or I play the clumsy card."

"So *that's* why you're always spilling your water bottle?" said T.D. "I was going to tell you to get a sippy cup."

"Wow, I had no idea you were doing that," said Helen.

"Me neither," said T.D. "You're my new hero!" He held up his hand for a high-five, but Alice didn't respond. She felt more like a *cero* than a hero.

"But, Alice," said Helen, "how hard can giving a speech in Spanish be?"

"Easy for you to say," said Alice. "You're practically bilingual!"

"I'm not bilingual," said Helen. "*Bilingual* means you speak two languages."

I wagged my tail. "I'm bilingual!" I announced.

But Helen went on. "I might understand more Spanish than you do

because my mom speaks it, but I'm not bilingual."

"I am!" I boasted. "I'm bilingual!"

"You don't speak Spanish, Martha," said Helen.

"No. But I can beg for ice cream in Human and in Dog. See?" I gave her my saddest puppy eyes and whined, *"Please?"*

Helen scratched my head. "You've got a point."

"Too bad you don't speak Spanish, Martha," said Alice. "You could help me with my speech."

Just then, Mom came in carrying baby Jake. Skits followed.

"Don't fill up," she warned. "Tío Jorge is cooking dinner tonight, remember?"

"He cooks Spanish food, right?" said T.D., looking over at Alice.

"No, not Spanish. Mexican," Mom said. "Helen's Uncle Jorge cooks the best Mexican food! *¡Deliciosa!* You're welcome to stay."

"Does he take requests?" T.D. asked.

"What did you have in mind?" Mom asked.

But T.D. just grinned mischievously.

# T.D.'S SOUPER SURPRISE

That evening, Mom was setting cooking utensils on the counter when a man's voice made her jump.

"DROP THAT LADLE!" he ordered.

"Agh!" Mom cried. She spun around to see Tío Jorge carrying a bag of groceries. He was with Helen's older cousin Carolina.

"*¡Hola*, Jorge! Carolina!" Mom said. "*¡Bienvenidos!*"

"You're not cooking tonight," he sang. "Tío Jorge is here!"

Carolina rolled her eyes in embarrassment. "Dad!"

"I brought everything," he said, placing his grocery bag on the counter. He pulled out fresh tomatoes. "Like *tomates frescos,* tortillas, and the ingredients for T.D.'s surprise."

Mom leaned in to see. "*¿Qué cosa?* What?"

But Tío Jorge crumpled the bag shut. "Oh, no! *¡Es un secreto!*"

"A secret?" Mom asked.

"That's right. Now *fuera, fuera,* out, out!" he said, scooting her out of the

kitchen. "Tío Jorge,"
he said dramatically,
"works alone!"

For the next hour,
he was a whirlwind of dicing, chopping,
stirring, and tasting. I hung around for scraps,
but he didn't drop anything. NOT A SINGLE
SCRAP, I TELL YOU!

Finally, Tío Jorge called, "Time to eat!"

We sat down to a feast. Well, I sat down
under the table.

"Enchiladas, chalupas, and T.D.'s super-secret request," he said, lifting the lid off a soup pot. "*¡Sopa de letras con albóndigas!*"

I licked my chops. "Is that Spanish for 'smells really good'?"

"No," said T.D. as Tío Jorge served the soup. "It's Spanish for 'alphabet soup with meatballs.' Right?"

"*¡Sí!*" Jorge replied. "Eat up!"

He placed a bowl in front of Alice. She eagerly dipped in her spoon. But just as she lifted it to her mouth, T.D. grabbed her arm.

"WHAT ARE YOU DOING?" he shouted.

"Uh, eating?" she said.

"YOU CAN'T! You're allergic to meatballs, *remember?*" T.D. winked.

"No, I'm not—"

"YOU'RE ALREADY GETTING A RASH!" he cried, yanking her to her feet. "Come outside. You need fresh air. I'll go with you."

"Huh?" said Alice.

He was carrying both of their bowls as he hurried her out the door.

The rest of us sat in confused silence.

"That," I said, "was strange."

Even stranger, T.D. poked his head back into the kitchen. "Martha," he said. "You come too!"

# "¿HABLO ESPANOL?"

I wanted to ask T.D. what he was up to, but I was too busy lapping up the soup he had given me. A dog doesn't ask questions when offered the gift of soup. *Mmm.*

T.D. dug in too, while Alice watched us eat.

"T.D.?" she yelled. "What are you doing?"

"Helping you," he said with his mouth full.

"Helping me?" Alice cried. She sat down and crossed her arms. "You could have at least given Martha *your* soup."

"Are you kidding?" T.D. said. "This soup is amazing. Besides, your oral report is due before mine."

Alice crossed her arms in exasperation. "What are you talking about?"

"Martha, speak!" T.D. ordered.

"¡*Hola!*" I said, and gasped. *Holy guacamole! Where did that come from?*

"*¡Sí!*" said T.D.

"*¿Sí?*" I said.

"See?" T.D. asked Alice.

"Not really," she said.

T.D. pulled a tape recorder from his pocket. "All you have to do is tell Martha what you want to say, record it, memorize it, then recite it—instant oral report."

Alice's eyes lit up. "AAAAAHHHHH!" she squealed, and batted T.D. on the shoulder. "T.D., you're a genius!"

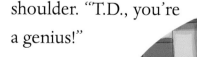

"Ouch." He winced. "I know." He handed Alice the tape recorder.

"Wait," she said. "This is such a great idea. Why aren't you using it yourself?"

T.D. thought for a moment. "Gah!" he said at last. "I don't know!"

"Well, thanks!" Alice said, and skipped back inside.

She didn't waste any time putting T.D.'s plan into action. After dinner, we went to her house.

"Okay, Martha," she said, sitting on her bed. "Whatever I say, you say it back in Spanish. Ready?"

"*¡Lista!*" I said.

From the windowsill, her awful cat Nelson let out a "HISS!" We didn't need a translator to know that was cat for "GO AWAY!" and "I DON'T LIKE THIS PLAN."

But Alice just giggled and held the tape recorder out toward me. "For my oral report, I'd like to talk about Mexican food," she said.

"*Para mi informe oral, quisiera hablar sobre la comida mexicana,*" I repeated in Spanish.

Alice beamed. "This is brilliant!" she said to herself. And then to me, "I LOVE Mexican food."

"*¡A mí también me encanta la comida mexicana!*" I said.

"Enchiladas. Chalupas. Carnitas," said Alice.

"*¡Enchiladas! ¡Chalupas! ¡Carnitas!*" I repeated.

"The end," said Alice.

"*El fin,*" I said.

Just then, T.D. arrived carrying a bowl of soup.

"Hey, guys!" he said, setting it in front of me. "I brought some of Granny Flo's alphabet soup so Martha can talk in English again once you're done."

"*¡Justo a tiempo!*" I said.

"Huh?" said T.D.

"Right on time!" I said, slurping it up. "All that talk about Mexican food made me hungry—and dog tired. Time to—"

"*HISS!*" went Nelson.

"Exactly," I said. It was time to go away.

Outside, T.D. and I waved goodbye to Alice.

"Thanks, Martha!" she called from her front porch. Next to her, Nelson growled.

"Nelson!" Alice scolded. "It's the only way I'm going to pass Spanish, okay?"

That night, she stayed up late to memorize her assignment. Despite Nelson's look of disapproval.

*Would she be ready?* I worried.

But when it was time to give her report, Alice didn't need anyone's help.

"*¡Enchiladas! ¡Chalupas! ¡Carnitas! ¡El fin!*" she said perfectly.

The class applauded. Helen and T.D. gave her a thumb's up.

"*¡Muy bien, señorita* Alicia! A-plus," said Señor Craig.

Alice offered a small smile. Something was bothering her, but she didn't know what it was.

# AMBASSADOR ALICE

Alice's A-plus was the talk of the town. She was front-page news. "Local Girl Passes Spanish Oral Exam with Flying Colors!" read the headline.

She quickly became an international Spanish-speaking sensation!

So when the U.S. ambassador to Mexico became too ill to work, Alice was asked to take his place.

On her first day, she sat at the head of a long table. She listened to the

Local Girl Passes Spanish Oral Exam with Flying Colors!

foreign ministers of Argentina and Mexico argue.

"*¡Sí!*" said one.

"*¡NO!*" said the other.

"*¡SÍ! ¡SÍ! ¡SÍ!*"

"*¡NO! ¡NO! ¡NO!*"

Finally, the Mexican foreign minister turned to Alice for help.

"Umm," she squeaked. "I think I should tell you something."

"*¿Sí?*" they asked.

"The fact is, I, uh, don't actually *understand* Spanish," Alice confessed.

The foreign ministers looked confused.

"How is this possible?" the Mexican foreign minister demanded. "You got an A-plus on your oral report."

"Well, it's like this," Alice said. "I memorized what the dog said and recited it. *Recite* means you say it out loud from memory. Like a nursery rhyme."

The Mexican foreign minister glared at her.

"Like a *nursery rhyme*? You mean ... *you cheated?*"

Alice smiled sheepishly.

The foreign minsters rose from their chairs. "Cheater, cheater, cheater!" they chanted.

Alice's stomach turned. She covered her ears. It was no use. All she could hear was the horrible truth: "CHEATER! CHEATER! CHEATER!"

# CHEATER!

"CHEATER! CHEATER! CHEATER!" the foreign ministers chanted in Alice's dream.

She sat up with a gasp.

"Ahh," she sighed, looking around. "It was only a dream."

By her bed, Nelson mewed accusingly. "*Meow.*"

"Okay! Okay!" said Alice. "I'll tell Señor Craig the truth."

The next day, after Spanish class, Alice slumped on a stool across from Señor Craig and told him everything.

"Let me see if I understand," he said, leaning against the desk. "The dog translated your words into Spanish and then you memorized—*memorizaste*—what the dog said?"

Alice nodded. "Yes, that's right. I cheated."

Señor Craig smiled. "Not really."

"Huh?" said Alice.

"You learned the way everyone learns," he said.

Alice looked shocked. "By taping talking dogs?"

Señor Craig laughed. "No. By memorization. When we memorize something, it means we learn it. Take the ABCs. We don't know them when we're babies. But our parents sing the song, and we repeat it, *lo repetimos.*"

Alice frowned. "Like a nursery rhyme. I know."

"Right," he said. "Then we start to connect the song with the letters—and presto! We've memorized, or learned, our ABCs."

Alice didn't seem convinced.

"Look at it this way," said Señor Craig. "What if I asked you: *¿De que trataba tu informe oral?*"

"Mexican food," Alice replied.

"*En español, por favor,*" he said.

Alice sighed. "*De la comida mexicana.*"

"*¿De verdad? ¿Te gusta la comida mexicana?*" Señor Craig asked.

"*Sí, me gusta mucho,*" said Alice.

"*¿Y cuál es tu favorita?*"

"I understand what you're saying!" Alice exclaimed. "*¡Me gustan las enchiladas!*"

Señor Craig spoke again. This time, he said twice as many words in half the time.

Alice held up her hand. "Don't get carried away," she said. "I'm not that good."

"Yet," said Señor Craig.

Alice grinned. "Yet."

As they walked out of class, she agreed to do a makeup report.

"Your *own* translation this time," said Señor Craig. "But at least it should be easier now. *¡Hasta luego!*"

"*Adiós*, Señor Craig," Alice replied.

And her Spanish was *perfecto*.

# MARTHA SAYS "ADIOS"

Well, *amigos,* that wraps up today's lesson. I hope you've learned a lot about dogs and teachers and dog teachers.

Next lesson: How to pretend you have a tail and chase it. (It's a doggone shame that humans don't have tails.)

Who knows? Maybe one day I'll be *your* substitute teacher.

Until then, keep studying, and on behalf of dogs everywhere, PLEASE stop blaming us for eating your homework. I mean, really! Dogs never blame kids for things. Okay, there was that one time I chewed part of the sofa and blamed Helen. Oddly, nobody believed me.

Er, now is probably a good time to say . . . Class dismissed!

*El fin.*

# GLOSSARY

**articulate:** to say something clearly

**attendance:** a reading out of students' names to find out who's in class and who's absent

**attention:** focus and careful listening

**behavior:** how a person or animal acts

**bilingual:** able to speak two languages

**memorize:** to learn by heart

**pronounce:** to say

**recite:** to say aloud from memory

**report:** a written or oral (spoken) presentation that tells people about a certain subject

**substitute:** someone or something that takes the place of someone or something else

# ¡OLÉ! A MEXICAN FIESTA

Tío Jorge knows how to make family meals fun. Plan a Mexican-themed dinner night with your family. Help out by rinsing lettuce or setting the table. Make festive placemats or a colorful menu by listing your dishes and drawing pictures to go with them. What will be on your menu?

*taco* (TAH-co) a fried, folded corn tortilla filled with meat, cheese, and veggie toppings

*quesadilla* (KAY-suh-DEE-yuh) a savory filling placed between two tortillas

*enchilada* (en-chi-LAH-dah) a tortilla rolled around meat and/or cheese and topped with a spicy sauce

*burrito* (burr-REE-toh) a flour tortilla wrapped around beans, meat, cheese, rice, and/or veggies

*fajita* (fah-HEE-tah) soft tortilla wrapped around fried strips of meat and veggies

*chalupa* (cha-LOO-pah) a fried tortilla in the shape of a boat with a spicy filling

*sopa de letras con albondigas* (SOAP-ah day let-ras con al-BON-dee-gas) alphabet soup with meatballs

*ensalada* (en-sah-LAH-dah) salad

*arroz* (arr-ROSS) rice

*frijoles* (free-HO-lays) beans

*queso* (KAY-soh) cheese

*pollo* (POH-yoh) chicken

*carnitas* (car-NEE-tas) shredded pork

*pan* (pahn) bread

*agua* (AH-gwah) water

*leche* (LAY-chay) milk

# Martha Says "¡Hola!"

Now you can speak and speak in Spanish just like Martha! Look here to find translations of the Spanish words used in the story. Practice saying these words and phrases, then try them out with your friends and family.

*Hola* (OH-lah) Hello

*Adiós* (ah-DYOSE) Goodbye

*¡Buenos días!* (BWAIN-ose DEE-ahs) Good morning!

*Hasta luego* (AH-stah LWAY-go) See you later

*Me llamo* (may YAH-mo) My name is

*Sí* (see) Yes

*No* (no) No

*Por favor* (pour fah-VORE) Please

*Gracias* (GRAH-syahs) Thank you

*De nada* (day NAH-dah) You're welcome

*¿Hablas inglés?* (HA-blahs ing-LACE) Do you speak English?

*¡Escuchen!* (es-KOO-chen) Listen up!

*amigo* (ah-MEE-go) friend

*lista* (LEE-stah) ready

*cero* (SAY-ro) zero